Book #1 in the *Becoming a Better You!* series

Are You Confident Today?

To Jack and Emma,
High 5 for Character!
Marian Nelson
and
Kris Yankee

FERNE PRESS

Written by Kris Yankee and Marian Nelson • Illustrated by Jeff Covieo

Are You Confident Today?
Becoming a Better You! series

Copyright © 2014 by Kris Yankee and Marian Nelson

Layout and cover design by Jacqueline L. Challiss Hill
Illustrations by Jeff Covieo
Illustrations created with digital graphics

Printed in Canada

Summary: Kids learn ways to be confident toward themselves and with others.

Library of Congress Cataloging-in-Publication Data
    Yankee, Kris and Nelson, Marian
    Are You Confident Today?/Kris Yankee and Marian Nelson–First Edition
    ISBN-13: 978-1-938326-24-0
    1. Confidence. 2. Self-esteem. 3. Character education. 4. Optimism. 5. Empathy. 6. Self-assurance.
    I. Yankee, Kris and Nelson, Marian II. Title
    Library of Congress Control Number: 2013956666

FERNE PRESS

Ferne Press is an imprint of Nelson Publishing & Marketing
366 Welch Road, Northville, MI 48167
www.nelsonpublishingandmarketing.com
(248) 735-0418

More Praise for *Are You Confident Today?*

"Socially and emotionally competent children are confident children. Kris Yankee's and Marian Nelson's new book, *Are You Confident Today?*, encourages children to reflect on their own confidence and think about taking risks to build their confidence. Without confidence, children are not able to take the risks necessary to develop the social and emotional skills they need to deal with their daily challenges. A variety of situations are presented that encourage the readers to think about their own lives and where they can practice being confident. Parents, teachers, and counselors will find that *Are You Confident Today?* opens the door to discussion and exploration of not only confidence but also discussions about self-esteem, peer relationships, and the daily challenges experienced by our children." ~Gary G. F. Yorke, Ph.D., Licensed Psychologist, President, childtherapytoys.com, LLC

"This book acts as a manual for how to help children become confident through good character building. *Are You Confident Today?* combines ideas like helping others, looking out for friends, and daily affirmations that reinforce one of the most important things we can do for our children: build their self-esteem." ~Nicholas Russo, Elementary Principal and Father of three

"Having worked with children for many years, I see great value in a book on confidence and character that combines a fun story, practical tips for both children and parents, and helpful discussion questions. We parents need all the help we can get in teaching our kids principles that will benefit them forever. *Are You Confident Today?* is a great read for children of any age."
~Christine Rossi, MSW, Counselor/Life Coach

Dedication

This book is dedicated to all of the great role models, parents, educators, and individuals who are committed to building healthy character in people of all ages. It is because of your loyalty to humanity that we will see the lasting results in our children. They will grow up to be positive role models for the next generation.

A special thank you to the staff at Nelson Publishing & Marketing, Patti, Kathy, Dawn, Amanda, and Jacqueline, for their ideas, suggestions, support, and vision for the future.

Every day is a new day. Today is about being confident.

When you're confident,
you believe in yourself and
what you can do.

Try this!
Each day when you wake up,
say out loud,
"I'm ready to do my best."

You can make your own breakfast.
Learn how to crack an egg into a frying pan.
In fact, you can make breakfast for your brother, too.

Wow, that's a great
start to your day.

You are organized! You pack your own backpack for school.
Your mom doesn't have to ask if you're prepared for the day.
She is confident you're ready.

If you're good at math,
you can help others with their homework before school.
By encouraging others to do their best,
you help build their self-confidence.

Hey! You're smart and know how to be confident in the classroom.
Raising your hand to answer a question,

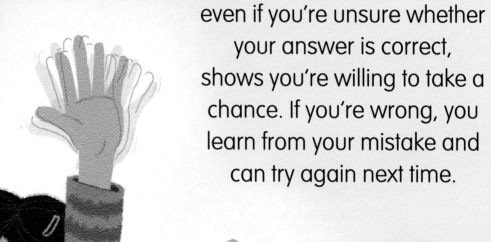

even if you're unsure whether
your answer is correct,
shows you're willing to take a
chance. If you're wrong, you
learn from your mistake and
can try again next time.

When your science teacher assigns a difficult partner project,
you're certain that it will turn out well because
you all work hard together.

When a friend is afraid to confront a person who is acting like a bully, you show support by standing by her side.

Have your friend practice what she's going to say,
so she feels prepared. If the problem is resolved,
you won't need an adult's help.

That's
empowering!

Trying something new can be very scary.
At first, you might question yourself and feel anxious.

Take a deep breath. Think positive thoughts and have courage. Remind yourself that you can do it.

Sometimes we think we have lost our confidence.
We might say things like, "I can't do it" or "I'm dumb."
Be careful!
Listening to those words will make you feel bad.
You won't achieve your goals
using words like "I can't."

Which Canadian province produces more than half of the country's manufactured goods?

Ontario

If your goal is to win the geography bee and you're nervous, remember how much you studied and know in your heart that you'll do the best you can. Practice will help you be successful.

Donating your time at a place like an animal shelter will help the puppies and kittens be happy.

You'll feel happy, too!

Raking leaves can be hard work,
but you're willing to help someone who can't do the job.
Confident people don't mind stepping up to do hard work.

When someone is trustworthy, honest, and caring,
you can rely on them to be a true friend.

A strong leader is also a confident person.
When you are chosen to be the captain or leader of your team,
be a good role model for the other team members.

Being confident doesn't mean that you're better than others.

Nobody's perfect.

STE-E-E-RIKE THREE!!!!

Putting others down is not how
a confident person behaves.
Remember to be supportive
when someone makes mistakes.

Decide to start today.
Acknowledge your own talents and abilities.

Practice becoming a better you.

Why do we need confidence?
When you have self-confidence, you will

• always give your best effort

• feel successful at school and other activities

• be comfortable trying new things

• believe in yourself

• not be afraid to work hard

• encourage others to do their best

• be a positive role model for others

• grow up to be a caring person

Now you know why confidence is important.
Life is happier and more fulfilling with a confident heart.

When you lay your head down on your pillow tonight,
remind yourself of all the ways you were confident today.
Remember that being confident takes practice.

Practice, practice,
and never give up.
Give yourself a big hug!

Reflections

- Name some times when you felt confident.

- What do you do if you wake up grumpy? How do you turn your mood around?

- Name three ways of taking care of yourself.

- What happens if you forget something for school or an activity and no one is available to bring it to you? Who is responsible for your belongings?

- Name someone who helped you. What did they do? Now is a great time for you to help someone else.

- Have you ever made a mistake and given up? What other choice could you have made?

- What's good about working with a partner?

- Have you ever been a bystander? A bystander is someone who watches bullying behavior and doesn't do anything.

- When was the last time you tried something new? Name two new things that you've tried recently.

- When you lost your confidence, what did you do to get it back?

- For your next volunteer opportunity, will you choose to help animals or people? Why?

- Whom do you consider to be a true friend? Why?

- How do you help others build their confidence?

- What do you do well? Make a list.

- In what areas in your life could you have more confidence?

Tips for Creating Confident Kids

- Encourage kids to DO their best, not BE the best.

- Teach kids to embrace their failures and use them as learning opportunities for the future.

- Have kids get out of their comfort zone and try new things. Whether they experience failure or success, they'll gain confidence in knowing that taking a risk can be beneficial.

- Encourage kids to solve problems on their own. Don't be afraid to step back and let kids make their own discoveries.

- Make kids responsible for their own belongings and for being prepared for school/sports/activities.

- Teach kids to have good posture. Standing up straight and looking directly at others when speaking helps them to establish themselves confidently in a conversation.

- Encourage your child to set goals. Keep a journal of goals and the outcome of each goal. Remind him/her that the result, good or bad, isn't the point in creating a goal—it's the journey toward the goal and what's learned that really matter.

- Set a good example by being a confident person.

Dear Reader,

It is our goal as parents and educators to help kids grow up to be confident and effective problem-solvers in this world. Can this be achieved? Families and schools around the globe are instituting programs that develop confident characteristics in children. *Are You Confident Today?* is a great tool to use in addition to any character program or to support family goals.

Why raise confident kids? It's simple: confidence breeds resilience. It's vital that our kids grow up healthy, both physically and emotionally. Without confidence, people can fumble through life, not fulfilling their purposes. Confident people make great leaders, care about the well-being of others, are trustworthy and respectful, develop their personal skills, and are more hopeful about the future.

We believe the world is a better place with happier, more confident people. Wouldn't you agree?

Kris Yankee and Marian Nelson

Author Biographies

Photo by Eric Yankee

Kris Yankee is a freelance editor, writer, wife, and mom. Kris feels blessed to have been able to be a part of this new series, as she believes that the values presented are those that she hopes to instill in her own children. She is an award-winning author of *Cracking the Code: Spreading Rumors* and *Tommy Starts Something Big: Giving Cuddles with Kindness* co-written with Chuck Gaidica. For more information about Kris, please visit her at facebook.com/BooksbyKrisYankee.

For the last nine years, Marian Nelson has been the publisher for Nelson Publishing & Marketing. She is happy to launch this new series of books called **Becoming a Better You!** Helping people grow to become better individuals has been her life passion. Formerly an educator for nearly twenty years, Marian keeps her focus on the children of the world, actively pursuing concepts of building healthy character. She continues to reach out to as many as possible in her talks and books. It is her hope that people will focus on learning and growing from the concepts presented in this book series and to work on self-improvement.

Visit us at nelsonpublishingandmarketing.com • parentsforcharacter.blogspot.com
• facebook.com/pages/Nelson-Publishing-Marketing

Illustrator Biography

Jeff Covieo has been drawing since he could hold a pencil and hasn't stopped since. He has a BFA in photography from College for Creative Studies in Michigan and works in the commercial photography field, though drawing and illustration have been his avocation for years. *Are You Confident Today?* is the seventh book he has illustrated.